Please return or renew this item before the latest date shown below

Renewals can be made
by internet   www.onfife.com/fife-libraries
in person   at any library in Fife
by phone   03451 55 00 66

ON
AT FIFE
LIBRARIES

Thank you for using your library

Thank you for using your library

For Anna, always full of bounce! Love ~ T C

For Teddy Tops ~ C P

LITTLE TIGER PRESS
1 The Coda Centre,
189 Munster Road, London SW6 6AW
www.littletiger.co.uk

First published in Great Britain 2013
This edition published 2013
Text copyright © Tracey Corderoy 2013 • Illustrations copyright © Caroline Pedler 2013
Tracey Corderoy and Caroline Pedler have asserted their rights to be identified as the author
and illustrator of this work under the Copyright, Designs and Patents Act, 1988
A CIP catalogue record for this book is available from the British Library
All rights reserved

ISBN 978-1-84895-540-0
LTP/1400/0758/1013
Printed in China
2 4 6 8 10 9 7 5 3

BOO!

Tracey Corderoy • Caroline Pedler

LITTLE TIGER PRESS
London

Hullabaloo was playing his **favourite** game.
He hid, as quiet as a mouse, and waited,
and waited, **then** . . .

Doinggggg!
went his ears.

Wiggle-waggle!
went his tail, **and** . . .

"BOO!"
cried Hullabaloo, jumping out.

"Arrggh!" shouted Squirrel, falling into a puddle.

Splish-
Splosh-
Splat!

And off raced Hullabaloo to surprise **another** friend.

He tiptoed up
to Hedgehog...

"**BOO!**" giggled
Hullabaloo.
"Oooo!" gasped
Hedgehog, toppling
on to the floor.

Crash!

But Hullabaloo
had already
bounced off
to surprise
Timid Mouse.

"**BOOO!**"

hooted Hullabaloo...

"Eeeeeeeeeeek!"
squeaked Timid Mouse.
And he cried and
cried and
cried . . .

"Oh, sorry!" gasped
Hullabaloo. "I didn't mean
to scare you!"
"Well," sniffed
Timid Mouse,
"you did."

"You're just too bouncy,"
Squirrel sighed.
   "And noisy," Hedgehog
grumbled. "No more boos
from you, Hullabaloo!"
   Hullabaloo gulped.
"What, no more boos at all?"
he said.

"No more
boos!"

So Hullabaloo tried his best
not to boo.

Doing*ggggg*!

went his ears when
Squirrel skipped by.

But he **didn't** boo...
"Ooooooooo!"

Wiggle-waggle!

went his tail when the others walked past.

He curled up small, **really**, **really** trying not to boo, until . . .

"Boo hoo hoo!"

blubbered Hullabaloo.

"Poor Hullabaloo," said Timid Mouse.
"Don't be sad, it's your birthday tomorrow!"
"But I **love** playing boo," sniffed Hullabaloo,
"especially on my birthday!"

"All right," Hedgehog smiled, "tomorrow
you can boo all day long."
"Really?" said Hullabaloo. "**Hooray!**"

The next morning, Hullabaloo bounced out of bed. "**It's my birthday!**" he cheered. "**Time to boo!**"

He hurried off to surprise his friends . . .

"**BOO!**"
cried Hullabaloo.

"BOO!"

yelled Hullabaloo.

pop!

"**BOO!**" whispered Hullabaloo. "**Whoo hoo!** See you at my party!"

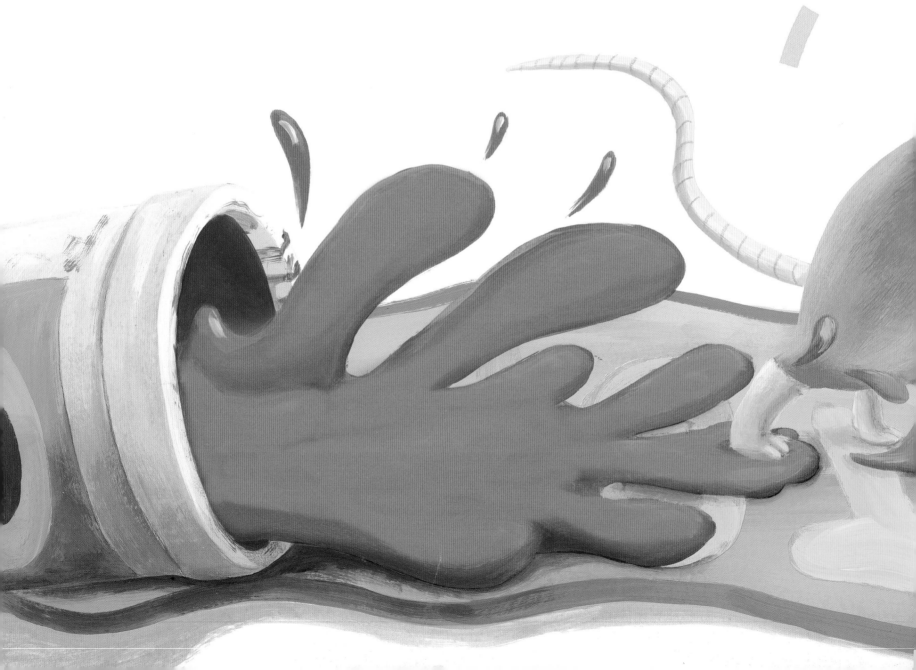

Hullabaloo's friends shook their heads.

"Look at the mess!"
Squirrel said.

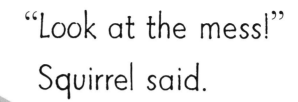

"The party
things are ruined,"
sighed Hedgehog.

"He didn't mean it,"
squeaked Timid Mouse.
"He's just too excited.
Don't worry — we can still
make his party special!"

And he whispered
a plan to the others...

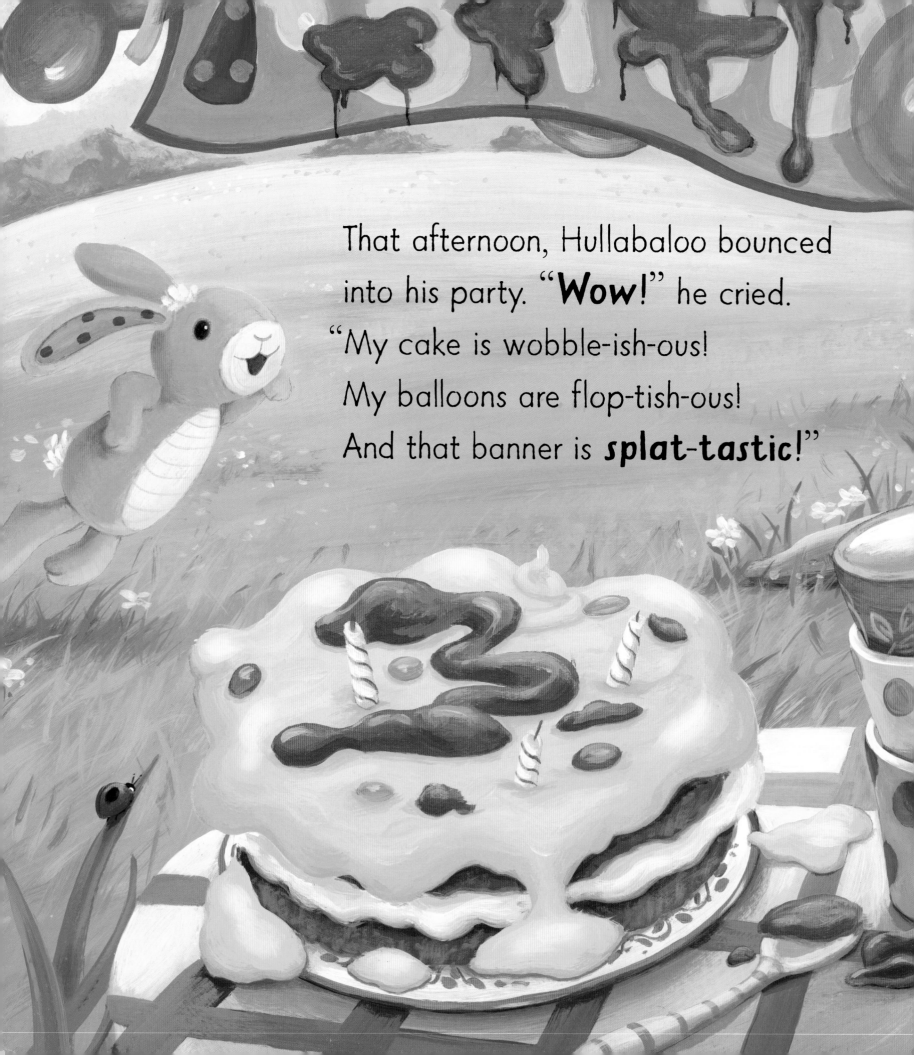

That afternoon, Hullabaloo bounced
into his party. **"Wow!"** he cried.
"My cake is wobble-ish-ous!
My balloons are flop-tish-ous!
And that banner is **splat-tastic!**"

Suddenly, Hullabaloo stopped. "But where are my friends?" he said. "**Oh no!** I must have been too noisy again and now no one is coming!"

Hullabaloo was about to go home, all on his own, **when** ...

"Hee hee!" giggled Hullabaloo.
"What a **BOO**tiful surprise!"
Then everyone joined Hullabaloo in
a big, birthday game of
BOO!

More **boo**tiful books from Little Tiger Press!

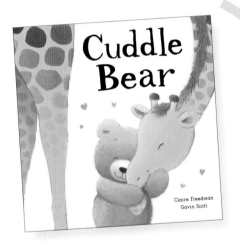

Cuddle Bear

Claire Freedman
Gavin Scott

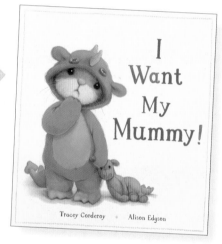

I Want My Mummy!

Tracey Corderoy • Alison Edgson

I'm NOT SLEEPY!

Jane Chapman

NO!

Tracey Corderoy
Tim Warnes

Super-Duper Dudley!

Sue Mongredien
Caroline Pedler

Bear's Big Bottom

STEVE SMALLMAN & EMMA YARLETT

For information regarding any of the above titles or for our catalogue, please contact us:
Little Tiger Press, 1 The Coda Centre, 189 Munster Road, London SW6 6AW
Tel: 020 7385 6333 • Fax: 020 7385 7333 • E-mail: info@littletiger.co.uk • www.littletiger.co.uk